Ferdie the Fly

By **Donald Gent** and Retold by **Rachel Ruth**

www.IntellectPublishing.com

Copyright © 2020 Rachel Ruth

ISBN: 978-1-945190-94-0
www.FerdieTheFly.com

FV-12

Contents

Ferdie at the Birthday Party

A family of flies lived inside a post near an ice cream store. They loved their home because the ice cream man came out every day and placed a scoop of ice cream on the top of the post for them to eat. Ferdie and his family liked the ice cream very much, and every day they would lick it until it was all gone.

One day the owner was late bringing ice cream out, and Ferdie

became very hungry and told his parents he wanted to go find something to eat.

"The world is a very dangerous place," his father said. "People might try to hit you with fly swatters or chase you down with rolled-up newspapers."

"Oh, I'll be careful," Ferdie said, as he flapped his wings and left the post.

He flew and flew until finally, he saw a house below him. He was very tired and needed to rest, so he landed upon a windowsill right outside a kitchen. He looked into the window and saw a woman mixing up something. He smelled food and boy did it smell good! So good, that it made his stomach churn.

What Ferdie didn't know was a birthday party was about to take place. The mom was starting to mix the cake dough. Ferdie had never seen dough, but that didn't matter because it still looked good enough to eat. The woman was ready to turn on the mixer when a little girl yelled from somewhere in the house. The mom dashed out of the kitchen to find the little girl, and Ferdie knew this was his chance. He had spotted a hole in the window screen and squeezed through it, then headed for the cake dough. He was licking the dough when the mom returned to the kitchen. She flipped the switch of the mixer on before Ferdie could get away, and he was caught up in a whirlwind of cake dough. Ferdie's head was spinning, and he felt dizzy and sick at his stomach. It seemed like he was moving 1000 miles an hour, and he was choking for air. The dough was in his eyes, his mouth, his nose, and his ears. He was stuck, and couldn't move his arms and legs. He pushed and tugged until he thought he would tear his legs off or his arms would come loose at their joints.

Oh my! My father told me to be careful and now I'm in a terrible mess, Ferdie thought.

"Help, help!" he yelled but there were no other flies around to rescue him.

Then the mixer stopped, and he thought, this is my chance to escape. Before he could wiggle free, the girl's mom poured the cake dough into a pan, and all of a sudden Ferdie could feel the heat from the oven. Whoa, it got hotter and hotter and hotter! Sweat was running down his

face, arms, and legs. He could hardly stand the intense heat. He thought this was the end, and he started to cry because he was so afraid. The time in the oven went on and on until Ferdie passed out.

Ten little girls came to the birthday party. The cake was beautifully decorated with 10 candles, and the table was decorated with streamers and balloons. All the little girls gathered around for a piece a cake. The mom cut the first piece of cake for the birthday girl, and the knife sliced right beside Ferdie's ear. The little girl saw the fly in her piece of birthday cake and started to cry. The noise made Ferdie wake up, and he looked around at all the children. He worked himself free, then shook his wings and started to fly straight for the hole in the window screen to escape.

Meanwhile, the little girl was sad that her birthday party had been ruined by Ferdie, but her mom surprised her.

Don't cry honey, I had enough cake dough for two cakes, and it'll only take a couple of minutes to frost the second one," she consoled her as she patted her on the back.

So, the party turned out just fine, and the little girls had a lot of fun.

Poor Ferdie, he was flying as fast as he could to get away from that party. He flew and flew until he looked below and saw the ice cream store, and his home on the post.

His parents were waiting, because they'd been worried about him. He cried as he told them about how scared he was when he got stuck in the cake dough and baked in the oven.

His mother patted him on the head and said, "Ferdie it's okay, don't cry. You are home and safe now."

Then the owner of the ice cream store came out and placed some ice cream upon the post and they happily ate every drop.

THE END

One morning Ferdie's mom sent him and his sister outside to look for crumbs. She told them to gather as many as they could because she needed to make their dinner. Ferdie and his sister decided to search on top of the picnic tables first, but when they didn't find much, they went to look on the ledge at the front of the ice cream store where people order food.

They hadn't found many crumbs when Ferdie's sister gave up and decided to go home. Ferdie

9

told her to take the crumbs they'd found, and he would keep on looking.

He flew and flew around, before he spotted a trash can. He was tired from flying and needed a rest, so he landed on the rim of the can. He saw some food mixed in with the papers, and decided to taste it before he gathered some crumbs for his mom. He was licking the food when something hit him. At first, he thought, perhaps a person had hit him with a newspaper. So, he glanced out of the corner of his eye and saw a big bully fly sitting on the rim shaking his fist at him.

Ferdie was surprised and yelled, "Why did you hit me?"

"You are in my can, eating my food, so leave it alone," sneered the bully fly.

"I've been flying around, and got hungry and needed something to eat," Ferdie explained.

The bully fly stomped his feet and said, "I don't care. Just get away from my food."

Ferdie stood up to the bully fly and said, "I didn't see you here when I landed."

"Well, if you don't leave, I will hit you again," the bully fly told Ferdie.

Ferdie continued to eat and watch the bully fly from the corner of his eye. His parents had taught him not to fight, but not to let anyone push him around either. In a flash, the bully fly came towards Ferdie, but he was ready. He doubled up his fist and socked the bully fly in the eye.

"I'm not scared of you, so leave me alone," Ferdie belted out.

The bully fly was startled because he thought Ferdie would leave, so he yelled, "You'd better leave or I'll get my friends."

Ferdie kept eating as he watched the bully fly take off. Then he thought to himself, I better go find my friends.

So he gathered up all his buddies until there were enough to make an army. He asked them to wait for him until he gave them the signal, and then he landed on the rim of the trash can. The bully fly and his friends were eating the food Ferdie had found, and that made Ferdie mad. He yelled, "Get away from my food."

"I thought you got scared and went home to your mommy and daddy," the bully fly said as he taunted Ferdie.

"Get away from my food, or you'll be sorry," Ferdie yelled as he felt his face turning red.

The bully fly and his friend mocked Ferdie as they continued to eat the food. Suddenly, Ferdie whistled through his teeth to send a signal to his army of friends, and they swooped in and pinned the bully fly and his friends to the papers, smearing the food on their faces. The bully fly and his friends didn't know what happened, but they were out of there in no time and never gave Ferdie any more problems.

Ferdie flew as fast as he could across the parking lot to tell his parents what had happened. He thought he would be in trouble when he told them he'd been in a fight with a bully fly.

"I didn't start the fight. Do you believe me?" he asked his mom as she wiped the crud off his wings.

"Sure, I believe you, but fighting is very dangerous. You want to avoid fighting, if at all possible."

"I tried to avoid it, but the bully fly came at me, and I had to protect myself. Then he went to get his friends, and they were going to beat me up," Ferdie said in between breaths. "I went and got my friends, and they helped me stand up to the bully. They had my back, and that bully fly won't be bothering me again," he further explained.

Ferdie's dad stepped in, patted Ferdie on the back and said, "We aren't upset with you, son. We just want you to be careful. You could've been hurt, and we don't want that."

Then his dad turned to go inside, and out of the corner of his eye, he saw the ice cream man coming to put ice cream on the post and thought it couldn't have come at a better time.

The End

Ferdie and the Toothpaste

The sun was shining, and it was a beautiful day. Ferdie wanted to go outside and play around at the ice cream store before it opened, so his mom told him to stay close and once it opened, he was to come home. By the time the ice cream store opened, the sun was blistering hot, and Ferdie was not only thirsty but he'd worked up an appetite. He wanted to go find something to eat, so he asked his dad if he could look for some food.

Ferdie's dad told him, "The world is a dangerous

place for little flies, so be very careful."

"I'll be careful," he told his father as he flapped his wings and took off from the post.

Ferdie flew and flew until finally, he saw a house below him. He was very tired and needed to rest, so he landed on the windowsill by an open window. He saw a man in his pajamas brushing his teeth. He didn't know what the man was doing, because he'd never seen anybody brushing their teeth before.

It fascinated him so much that he flew inside and landed upon the ceiling, so he could watch the man up close. After the man in the pajamas was finished, he took a drink of water and left. That's when Ferdie noticed an interesting looking tube on the edge of the sink. He'd never seen anything like it, and he wondered why the man left it there.

Ferdie whispered to himself, "This is my chance," and he flew down from the ceiling and curiously landed on the tube, and after a quick survey, he noticed some white gooey stuff that had stuck to his feet. The white gooey stuff smelled good, and he had a strong desire to taste it. So, he licked it with his tongue and it was delicious. Then he saw that the man in his pajamas had left the cap off, so he followed his nose which led him inside the opening of the tube.

It was dark inside the tube, but Ferdie didn't think about it being dangerous. He was more interested in the sweet taste of the toothpaste. Then out of nowhere, a woman came to clean the bathroom and saw the cap to the toothpaste had been left off, so she quickly screwed it back on, and tossed the tube into the drawer. Poor Ferdie bounced around when the tube hit the bottom of the drawer. He tried to find his way out, but it was like a dungeon inside the tube. His feet and his hands were stuck down in the gooey stuff, and he couldn't move or breathe very well. He pushed and pulled until he thought his legs and arms would pop out of their joints. Then he thought about his family, and how his father tried to warn him of the dangers.

He started to cry, but the people couldn't hear him, and there were no flies to help rescue him. He yanked and

yanked his legs until his feet were freed from the goo and then he laid down from pure exhaustion and went to sleep.

Ferdie had a rude awakening the next morning when the man in the pajamas grabbed the tube and squeezed it. Ferdie shot out with a stream of toothpaste and surprised

the man. He shook his toothbrush and flung it halfway across the room at Ferdie who had started flapping his wings and was heading for the window but it was closed. Ferdie made a quick u-turn, as the man picked up his newspaper and swung it at him. Ferdie dodged the newspaper and flew out of the bathroom. He flew down a long hall that led to the kitchen,

and there saw the woman had cracked the kitchen window for some fresh air. He jetted by her and escaped out into the morning air where he flew as fast and far away as he could from the danger.

"Whew," he said to himself as he looked down and saw the ice cream store.

He saw his parents and sister waiting for him on top of the pole where they live. He could tell they were worried, because Ferdie had never stayed overnight anywhere without his parents. When he landed, Ferdie told them about being caught inside the toothpaste tube, and how scared he was because it was dark.

His mother patted him on the head and said, "Oh, Ferdie, please don't cry. You are home safe now."

Then the ice cream man came out and placed some ice cream on top of the post and Ferdie and his family ate it all as they celebrated his safe return.

The End

Ferdie gets Saved

Ferdie was in his bedroom waiting for the ice cream man to come out and put ice cream on top of the post where he and his family lived, but the man never came. Ferdie thought that was odd because the man came every day. So, the next morning he decided to investigate. He flew to the front of the store and heard one of the workers say the ice cream man was on a trip and he'd be gone three days. He flew back home and told his parents and his sister.

His mom said, "Well, surely, one of the workers will bring us out some ice cream."

Ferdie and his family waited all day, but no one ever brought out any ice cream. The ice cream man must have forgotten to tell someone to put ice cream on the post. There was no ice cream the next day, or the next, and Ferdie was rubbing his stomach when he told his mom, "I am so hungry. I've got to go out and find something to eat."

His mom patted him on the back, and told him, "You've got to be careful because danger lurks everywhere, so keep your eyes open at all times."

"Oh, I will mom," Ferdie replied as he took off flying in the sky. He flew and he flew until he spotted a building with lots of cars around it.

Ferdie said, "Boy, there must be something going on down there. I've got to go take a look."

He flew down to take a closer look through a window and saw it was a church full of people running around with dishes full of food. When a man and woman walked toward the door, Ferdie decided, this is my chance. So, he landed on the man's back and went inside the church. Ferdie thought he'd gone to heaven because there was a long table with all kinds of dishes full of food on it. He headed straight for the potato salad and he started eating and eating until someone saw him and chased him away. With his mouth full, he flew up above the table and landed on a big support beam.

After all the people got their plates full and sat down, Ferdie swooped in again and went straight for the pasta salad. He was licking and licking the pasta when some lady came with a flyswatter and shooed him away while she covered up all of the food.

Then all the people started going into another room and he wondered where they were going, and so he followed them. They went into the sanctuary, and he wondered what they were going to do in there. There was a man up in the front with his back to everyone, doing funny things with his arms while the choir was singing. All the people were finding places to sit down on the longest benches Ferdie had ever seen.

These benches were much longer than the ones by the picnic tables at the ice cream store. Ferdie was looking for a safe place to sit down and watch the people. Then he saw a window that was made with all different colors of beautiful glass, so he flew up by it and sat down. He was curious to see what the people would do next. The people stood up, then they sat down and the preacher got up. He preached, and preached, and preached until some of the people fell asleep, but not Ferdie. When the preacher was done, he invited anyone to come to the front of the church who wanted to ask Jesus to come into their hearts.

Ferdie left where he was sitting by the pretty window and came down where he found a place to sit on the edge of the altar. There he asked Jesus to come into his heart and he got saved. Then before all the people could leave the church, he flew back into the dining hall and found a spot where he could eat some more food before heading home. Ferdie flew and he flew until he saw the ice cream store, and his mom and dad on top of the post.

He'd been gone a long time and he told his parents that he went to church, and got to know Jesus. He told them he wanted them to go with him next week, so he could introduce them to Jesus.

So, the next Sunday, Ferdie and his family flew over to the church and sat up by the beautiful stained-glass window and listened to the preacher.

After he preached and preached, Ferdie's family all got saved, just like him. They were the first flies that were ever saved, and they turned out to be missionaries.

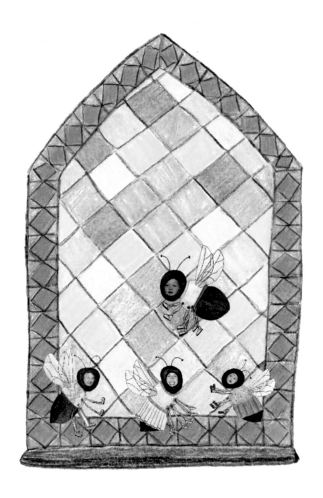

The End

Ferdie goes on Vacation

Ferdie woke up hot and knew it was going to be another blistery summer day. He found his mom in the kitchen and told her for the first time ever he wasn't hungry. She thought he was sick, but he wasn't. He was just too hot to have an appetite, and he needed to find a cool place to hang out.

Ferdie told his mom, "The ice cream store isn't open yet, and I want to go out and relax in the cool grass under the picnic tables before people start coming for ice cream."

"That's fine with me, but come back home when the ice cream store opens," she instructed him as she continued to make breakfast.

Ferdie put on his shoes and took off into the air, but it was hard to fly because the air was hot and sticky, and made him sweaty. He landed on one of the picnic tables to wipe down his wings when he noticed a little girl coming out of her house. She was pulling a big suitcase behind her, and then her dad took it and put in a big box on top of their station wagon. Then her two brothers came out with their suitcases and the
dad put them in the big box on top of the station wagon too.

Then the mom came out and opened the back of the station wagon, and started loading it with blankets and boxes.

Ferdie wondered what all the commotion was about, so he flew over and landed on the back bumper of the car to get a closer look. The kids got in the backseat, and the dad turned on the air conditioner for them while they waited for their mom. The air conditioner blasted, and Ferdie followed the inviting waves of cool air into the back of the car and

laid down. He was enjoying the cool air so much, that he missed getting out before the back door was closed. He felt the car moving and jumped up on the backseat just in time to see them drive past the ice cream store.

Ferdie said to himself, "I'm in trouble now." He wondered where they were going, and how he was going to get home. Ferdie sat down between the boxes and cried until he fell asleep.

He woke up when he heard all the car doors opening. The family was getting out, and he wondered where they were going. Then Ferdie saw it: a big arch. It was tall and looked like it could touch the sky. He wanted to get closer to it, so he zoomed out of the car and followed the family up the hill. The family went inside the big arch, but Ferdie didn't follow them. Instead, he took off and flew up and up and up, until he landed on top of the big arch.

Whoa! Looking down made him dizzy, but he could see a river, tall buildings, and crowds of people that looked little bitty. All this excitement made him realize he was hungry and needed to find some food. So, he flew down and found a little boy who shared a French fry with him. As he was eating, he saw the family he came with walking towards the car. Ferdie quickly washed his hands and face, and flew over to stay close to them, because they were his ride home. When the kids climbed in the car, so did Ferdie and they didn't even notice.

The mom fixed sandwiches and passed around a bag of potato chips for everyone to eat while they drove down the road. Ferdie found plenty of crumbs to fill his belly, and soon got tired and climbed into the back to sleep. He must have slept all night because the sun was rising when he woke up and they were still driving. He needed to stretch his wings and was hoping they would stop soon.

Finally, the car stopped and the kids woke up and started screaming with excitement. Ferdie didn't understand until he looked out the window and saw the ocean. He'd never seen a real ocean before, only a picture in a book. The dad got out and opened up the box on top of the car to get their suitcases, and the mom opened the back door to grab the blankets.

Ferdie knew this was his chance to get out, and he took flight into the warm and salty ocean air. He found a sand dune to lay on, and he watched the family build a sandcastle, and play in the waves. They played on the beach for two long days, while Ferdie followed them around and ate their leftovers.

Then it was time to leave, and Ferdie slipped into the car for the long drive home. They drove all day and all night before they pulled into their driveway. The family was so tired, that they didn't even notice Ferdie looking out the window at the ice cream store and post where his family lived. When the little girl opened her car door, Ferdie flew out as fast he could. He saw his parents sitting on top of the post, and he shouted, "Mom and Dad!"

They jumped up as Ferdie flew straight into their arms, and he told them about going on vacation with the family across the street. He talked so fast that he got the hiccups, and his mom asked him, "You know the best way to get rid of hiccups?"

"Eating ice cream," Ferdie answered, and hoped the ice cream man would come out soon to put a scoop of ice cream on top of their post.

The End

One morning Ferdie woke up very early when it was still dark outside. He couldn't sleep because he was cold, so he got up out of bed. He decided to go out to the kitchen and get something to drink when he noticed his dad sitting in his chair reading a book.

"What are you doing up so early, Ferdie?" his dad asked.

"I don't know. I just woke up and couldn't sleep. I guess I was kind of cold," he told his dad.

"Well, come over here and sit by me while I read," his dad suggested.

Ferdie sat down for a while, but he was still cold and he kept looking outside at one of the street lamps that was shining down in the parking lot. He thought how warm it had to be, and the more he thought about the warmth the more he wanted to sit under it. Finally, he peeked over his dad's book, and asked, "I'm still cold, so do you mind if I go outside and sit under that street lamp so I can get warm?"

"I guess not, Ferdie, but stay close to the light where it is safe."

So, Ferdie flew out by the street lamp and landed on the pole beneath it. He was enjoying the heat on his back when he noticed a big 18-wheeler parked in the lot of the ice cream store. He flew over to get a closer look and noticed one of the windows was cracked open, so he slipped inside and landed on the steering wheel.

As Ferdie's eyes adjusted, he saw a piece of hamburger laying on one of the seats. He said to himself, "What a great breakfast this would be."

He quietly glided down and started eating the piece of hamburger, when a man slowly crawled out from behind the seats.

Afraid to fly because the man might see him, Ferdie tiptoed across the passenger seat and hid behind it. The driver got up in his seat, turned the engine on, and rolled up the window.

Ferdie yelled, "Wait, I can't go with you. I've got to go home," but the man couldn't hear Ferdie yelling because the engine was too loud.

Ferdie had never taken a ride in a truck before, and he wondered if he could fly in midair while this truck was moving? Every few hours the driver would stop and get gas and food to eat in the truck, and leave Ferdie a few crumbs. Ferdie never tried to escape because he didn't know his way home. He hoped the man in the truck would make a big circle and take him back to the ice cream store, but instead, the man drove and drove. Sometimes he even stopped along the way to crawl in the back of the cab and go to sleep.

At times, Ferdie would lay his head down on his arms and cry, because he was lonesome for his parents. He wondered if they were looking for him. He had really messed things up this time and was tired of riding in this truck. Even though the scenery was beautiful, and Ferdie got to see the mountains, the Painted Desert, and the Grand Canyon, he was hot and just wanted to go home. He kept yelling at the driver to stop driving, but the driver couldn't understand fly talk.

Finally, they arrived in California. Ferdie knew that's where they were, by the picture books his mom read to him and his sister. There was the ocean, palm trees, and the HOLLYWOOD sign. They didn't stay in California long, because when the truck was unloaded, they were back on the road. It was the longest ride Ferdie had ever taken on their

way back, and he had to keep hiding from the driver who had seen him.

The driver would swing newspapers at him and roll down the windows and try to push him outside, but Ferdie hung on for dear life in hopes of going home.

At last, the big truck stopped, and Ferdie dashed out of the truck and started flying as fast as he could to get away from the man.

He flew and flew until he saw the ice cream store and his home on the post. His parents were waiting because he had been gone for days. This was the longest Ferdie had ever been gone from his dad and mom, and as he landed, they jumped with joy to see him.

Ferdie told them about being caught in the truck and how scared he was on the trip to California. His mom put her arm around his shoulders and said, "Ferdie, we're glad your home, and back in one piece."

Then his dad told him, "Ferdie, you're grounded for two weeks, and are not allowed to go outside and play by yourself."

"Okay," Ferdie answered because he was so glad to be home, "but, can I still have ice cream every day?"

"Yes, you can eat ice cream with the family," his dad told him.

Then the ice cream man saved the day when he put some ice cream on top of the post, and Ferdie and his family licked up every last sticky drop until it was gone.

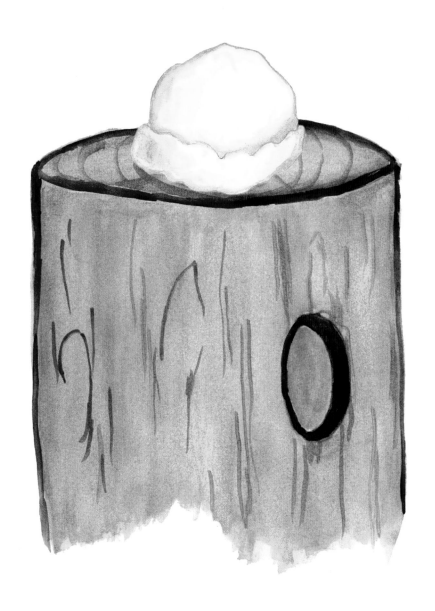

The End

Ferdie woke up on a Saturday morning at the crack of dawn with a boost of energy. He flew around the house trying to be quiet, but he eventually woke everyone up. He asked his sister to play, and soon they were buzzing around when their mom said, "Kids, you're being too rowdy, so go outside and play."

Ferdie and his sister happily made for a quick exit into the fresh morning as their mom reminded them, "Stay close by, so I'll be able to find you when I get

your breakfast made."

Ferdie and his sister flapped their wings and soared over the parking lot and landed on the nearest picnic table to search for leftovers as they enjoyed the sun on their backs.

Then they flew over to the front of the ice cream store and landed on the window to see if anyone was there, but it was too early. After a while, they got tired of playing and flew back to check on their breakfast, but their mom told them it wasn't quite ready.

Ferdie told his parents, "I'm going back outside."

"Well, don't stray too far. The ice cream store will be opening soon and people will be coming. Remember what I've told you about how dangerous it can be out there," Ferdie's dad told him as he drank his morning coffee.

"I know, Dad. I'll be careful."

Ferdie flapped his wings and flew outside. He flapped his way around the parking lot three times before he strayed. Soon, Ferdie had flown a long way from home, and when he looked down, he saw an amusement park below.

The park was just opening, and there were moving objects everywhere and people all over the place. He didn't even know what to look at first. All the people were laughing and having fun, and Ferdie didn't want to miss out on any of the excitement.

He got a whiff of something that smelled really good, and his stomach was full of rumbles, so he decided to swoop down and take a look. Guess what he saw? It was a food booth that made cotton candy. While the man was selling a cone of cotton candy, Ferdie decided to land at the bottom of the big pan to take a taste. He was licking the sugar as fast as he could when the man turned on the machine and Ferdie was caught up in the swirls of sugar and the spinning of the cotton candy fluff. It was like a big spiderweb engulfing him. He could see through it, but he couldn't get out. Ferdie yelled, "Help, help," but there were no other flies around that could hear him or take the chance of getting stuck like him.

Then the man took a cardboard cone and put it down in the churning machine, and made the cotton candy wrap around. Ferdie was buried deep inside the candy cone the man handed to a little boy across the counter. He tried to wipe the candy away from his eyes and kick free, but finally ran out of breath and gave up. So, he settled back and filled his stomach with the pink candy.

In a few minutes, Ferdie heard a strange noise that he had never heard before. It sounded like a big motor and chain. Then he heard big and little people laughing and yelling. At first, it frightened him, because he thought someone had noticed him in the candy. He just wished he could understand their words. Then he felt a forward movement, and all of a sudden there was a downward thrust that took his breath away. Ferdie felt like his stomach was in his throat, and that he might get sick, but he still couldn't move because his wings were stuck in the candy. He thought the downward movement would never end. The people were screaming like crazy and laughing. Then all of a sudden, they were going upwards, then downwards, and upwards, and downwards.

Ferdie thought it would never end, but then on the last downward thrust, the little boy's cotton candy flew out of his hand and went flying through the air. It shook Ferdie loose when it hit the ground, and he stumbled out. He looked up and realized he had been on a huge roller coaster.

He asked himself, "How did I ever get myself into this mess?" as he licked his front feet and wiped off his face.

Then he flapped his wings a couple of times and took off for home. He flapped and flew, and flapped and flew away from the dangers of the amusement park. Then he saw the ice cream store and his parents waiting for him on top of the pole because he'd been gone all day.

When he landed, Ferdie told them about being caught up in the cotton candy machine, and how scared he was

during the roller coaster ride. His dad reminded him about the dangers of flying too far from home, as his mom hugged him and they all went inside to wait for the man at the ice cream store to put a scoop of ice cream on top of their pole.

The End

Ferdie gets Swallowed by a Frog

The sun finally peeked out from between the clouds after three days of steady rain, and Ferdie was itching to get outside and stretch his wings.

"Hey look, the sun is out, does that mean I can go outside?" Ferdie asked his mom and dad.

His mom went over to look outside and said, "Ferdie, I understand you need to fly and flap your wings, so you go right ahead. Just stay close by, so you can hear us call when the ice cream man comes to put ice cream on our post."

Ferdie didn't waste any time. He was out the door and gone. He flapped his wings and he flew and flew and flew. He flew around in circles until the circles got bigger and bigger. Ferdie got so tired of flying in circles that he had to find a place to rest.

When he landed, he was at the edge of a small lake in a park. There were a lot of people having picnics in the park, and their food smelled delicious. He looked around and found that someone had laid a chocolate cupcake down by the water, so he landed on it and started to lick the icing.

What Ferdie did not know, was frogs lived in the water along the banks of the lake. He heard a funny croaking noise, but he had never heard this sound before. Then he became more aware of the ribbit sounds all around him.

Ferdie would hear one nearby, and then hear one in the distance. It sounded like they were sending signals and talking to each other, and he didn't know what to think of it.

He thought maybe they were talking about him, but he would never know because flies can't understand frog talk.

Maybe the frogs were saying, "There's a fly in our midst, and we'd love to eat him."

Ferdie didn't know he was in danger, and he couldn't see the frogs because they were the color of the grass and mud.

He didn't know that if he got too close to one of the frogs, that one of their long and little tongues would shoot out like a lightning bolt and lap him up. For the time being, Ferdie was content eating his cake.

Then a nearby frog saw Ferdie, and in a flash, Ferdie was curled in the tongue of the frog and on his way to the frog's stomach. Oh, it was daylight for one moment, and a dungeon the next. He found himself in a very crowded small area, and he couldn't breathe or see. He didn't know where he was, but it was really smelly. He was surrounded by other flies, bugs, and grasshoppers. Ferdie kicked and jerked until his body ached and his legs cramped. He was exhausted and out of energy, and thought, There's no hope for me.

Then for some odd reason, the frog got sick and vomited up Ferdie, and all the other bugs in his stomach. Ferdie was lying on the ground in front of the frog when he realized he had been inside the frog's stomach.

A flash crossed his mind, and it was his dad telling him about the dangers of the world. With that memory, Ferdie jumped up and started flapping his wings as fast as he could to get away from the frog. He took off into mid-air flapping and flying in big circles until he could see the ice cream store and his home on the post.

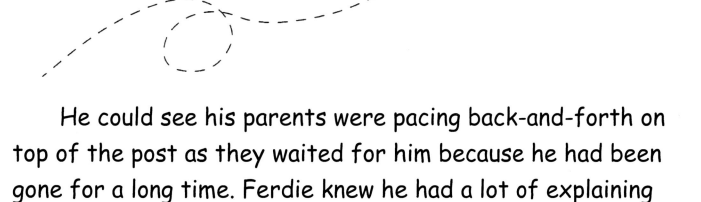

He could see his parents were pacing back-and-forth on top of the post as they waited for him because he had been gone for a long time. Ferdie knew he had a lot of explaining to do.

He said, "Dad, I didn't know about frogs or their long tongues. I didn't know I was in danger. I kept a lookout for the people that might swat at me, but the frog surprised me."

"There are lots of dangers in the world, son, when you're a fly. So, you always have to be aware of your surroundings."

About that time the ice cream man came out and placed some ice cream on top of the post and they licked it all up. Then they all went inside, and Ferdie got on his bed and took a nap.

The End

Ferdie goes to the White House

Early one morning, Ferdie was out flying around the ice cream store, when a big yellow bus pulled into the parking lot. He flew home to tell his mom and dad, and as he landed on top of the post, he yelled for them to come out. Ferdie and his family watched the bus door open, and one by one bunches of kids came out of the bus. The ice cream store had opened early and gave all the kids an ice cream cone. They ran and jumped and played while they ate their ice cream. Ferdie's family all watched until one boy

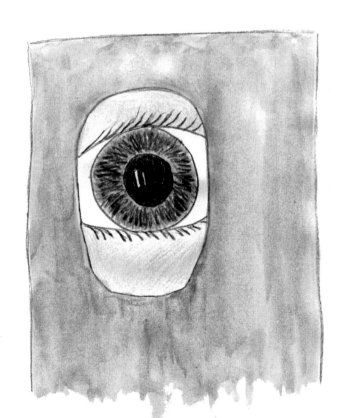

got too close to their post, and scared them back inside where they hid.

Ferdie heard the little boy say to another kid, "Hey, some flies just flew inside this hole," as he tried to look inside.

All Ferdie's family saw was a big eye looking in at them, so they ran back into their bedrooms. It was a good thing they did because the boy stuck his finger in the hole and knocked over their kitchen table. When Ferdie came out of his bedroom, the boy was gone and so was all the noise in the parking lot. Ferdie flew outside to see if they were gone, but they weren't yet.

All the kids were back on the bus, but the door was still open. So Ferdie flew as fast as he could across the parking lot and got on the bus. The kids were all busy talking, and the bus driver was looking at a map and didn't notice Ferdie when he flew in the open door. Ferdie flew high above all the kids' heads and landed at the top of the back window. No one had seen him, except for his parents who were standing on top of the post and waving their arms.

"Ferdie, get out of that bus before you get hurt," his mom shouted.

"You didn't ask to go anywhere. You need to come home right now, son!" Ferdie's dad yelled across the parking lot.

Before Ferdie could get out of the bus, the bus driver shut the door and Ferdie was trapped and looking out the window at his parents. As the bus pulled out of the parking lot Ferdie waved at his parents, and then flew up and landed on the ceiling above the kids. He decided not to buzz around because the boy with the big eye might spot him, and that thought scared Ferdie.

They rode for many hours until they came up to a big white building, where the bus driver parked and they all got out. Ferdie slipped through the door just before it was shut, and followed the kids. They met a man dressed in a fancy suit who said, "Welcome to Washington, D.C." Then he stepped up on some white steps and told them, "I'm your tour guide today, and we are going on a tour of the White House. You will need to walk in a single line and keep your voices down. We ask that you do not touch anything in the White House, including the walls."

Ferdie got in the back of the line and followed the kids through the big doors on the front of the house. Some of the kids put their hands in their pockets, but Ferdie didn't have any pockets. So, Ferdie flew close behind them trying not to touch anything. They stopped and stood in a room with the shiniest floors Ferdie had ever seen. The tour guide said the floor was made of marble tiles. They looked more like polished glass, and Ferdie thought if he was in his sock feet, he could've pretended to ice skate across them.

As they walked down a long hall and into several fancy parlors, Ferdie and the kids looked at many hand painted portraits of Presidents from long ago. Their tour guide told them the house was 200 years old, and that meant many presidents had lived there. Ferdie got the most excited when they went into the Oval Office, and he forgot about staying in line and took off flying in big oval circles until he made it up to a crystal chandelier where he landed. From there he could see everything, including a couch with some matching pillows. He flapped his wings and flew down, making a soft landing on one of the pillows, so he could take a quick nap. He'd only had his eyes shut for two minutes when one of the little girls found him and blew at him as hard as she could. Ferdie went into a midair tailspin and bounced off the shoulder of the tour guide. It knocked Ferdie silly for a few seconds as he landed on a table beside a silver bowl. He barely escaped the tour guide's hand, as he shook his head and flew off the table towards the hall.

He came to the top of the stairs when he spotted a brass banister and decided to slide down it for a quick

getaway. When he got to the bottom of the stairs, he saw their bus parked outside, so he flew over by the door and waited.

A few minutes later a Secret Service man opened the door and gave Ferdie just enough room to fly outside to the bus. Ferdie found one window that was slightly cracked, so he slipped inside the bus and hid under a seat where he fell asleep.

He must have been tired because he didn't even wake up when all the boys and girls got back on the bus. In fact, he didn't wake up until the bus stopped in the parking lot of school, where all the kids got off to meet their parents who were waiting to pick them up. Ferdie wished his parents were there, but they weren't and he knew the only way to find them was to start flying. He flew and flew until he saw the ice cream store and the post where his family lived.

Ferdie flew straight into the hole in the post where he was met by his parents. He told them all about going to the White House and falling asleep on a pillow in the Oval Office. His parents laughed so hard, that they forgot about being upset with Ferdie and they all went to bed at the end of another adventurous day.

The End

Ferdie goes in the City Sewer

Ferdie had eaten breakfast, read a book, and was playing games with his sister when he announced that he was bored. It was getting close to lunchtime, and Ferdie was hoping the man from the ice cream store would bring out some ice cream and put it on top of their post, but he didn't, so Ferdie decided that he would go out and find something to eat on his own.

"Dad and Mom, I'm gonna go outside and see if I can find something to eat," Ferdie told his parents as he put on his shoes. "I'll stay by the picnic tables, so you can see me," he added.

"Ferdie, you know what I always say; it's dangerous out there so keep your eyeballs open so nobody swats at you," his dad said in a stern tone.

"Okay, Dad I'll be careful,"
Ferdie said as he wiped off his
wings and took off.

Ferdie flew around all the picnic tables, until he spied a
French fry that someone had dropped on one of the
benches. He swooped in for a landing, but when he got a
little closer his heart dropped because it wasn't a French
fry after all. It was just a piece of a straw that some kid

had chewed off and didn't throw away. There was nothing around for Ferdie to eat on the picnic tables, so he decided to fly over to the house next door. After all, he told his Dad he would be careful and the house was close by.

Ferdie landed on the kitchen window and looked through the glass, and saw some dishes in the sink with food on them. It looked awful good, and Ferdie knew he had to find a way in, so he could eat it. He flew around the house looking for way to get in, but all the doors and windows were shut. He figured if he was going to get in the house, he'd have to go down the chimney. So, that's what Ferdie did.

He flew straight down the chimney, through the living room, and found the kitchen sink in no time. He was busy

licking up the food when a woman came into the kitchen, and turned on the faucet. Ferdie got caught in a flood of water,

and was quickly underwater and didn't know how to swim. He held his breath as he opened his eyes under the dishwater, and saw that he was headed straight for the drain. He didn't know how long he'd be able to hold his breath, and wondered how long he'd be swirling around and around.

Finally, the water stopped, and Ferdie was gasping for air while sitting inside a big black pipe. It was dark, and smelled terrible. He was so scared, and didn't know which direction was out. He decided to stay there for a little while to catch his breath, and that's when he heard a loud gushing noise that sounded like water coming through the pipes.

"Oh my!" Ferdie screamed as a flood of water picked him up and carried him to a new place on his way to the city sewer. The water stopped and left Ferdie stranded in the pipe. He was breathless from his trip for he'd been beneath the water the whole way. He laid on the pipe like a limp noodle, and coughed up the water that was still in his lungs and throat.

It seemed like hours before the next gush of water came down the pipe. Each gush of water got bigger and bigger, until Ferdie found himself in a very large pipe. It was full of nasty stuff, and Ferdie got sick three times. He wondered what his parents would say if they knew he was under the ground, lost in this big pipe. He had yelled until his throat was hoarse, but he was too far away for anyone to hear him and he thought he might have to live underground forever.

Then the largest gusher ever to come down the pipe was like a great flood. He didn't think he would survive this one. He didn't realize it was only a short way to the city sewer, and that he'd traveled through a network of pipes beneath the ground. He took a big breath, and waited to be carried away by the great flood, but to his surprise he surfaced and saw the sky. He was floating on a great pond of water, rubbish, and bad smelling stuff. Ferdie didn't waste any time, and started flapping his wings. He flew as fast as he could to get away from the dangers of the sewer. After he flew for a long time, he saw the ice cream store and his home at the post. He also saw a big scoop of ice cream on top of the post, and his family.

Ferdie landed and told them about being caught in the sewer, as tears streamed down his cheeks. His mom patted him on the head and said, "Ferdie, it's okay. You're home now. Eat your ice cream with us before it melts. It will make you feel better."

Soon Ferdie got full and he went inside and curled up on his bed and fell into a deep slumber.

The End

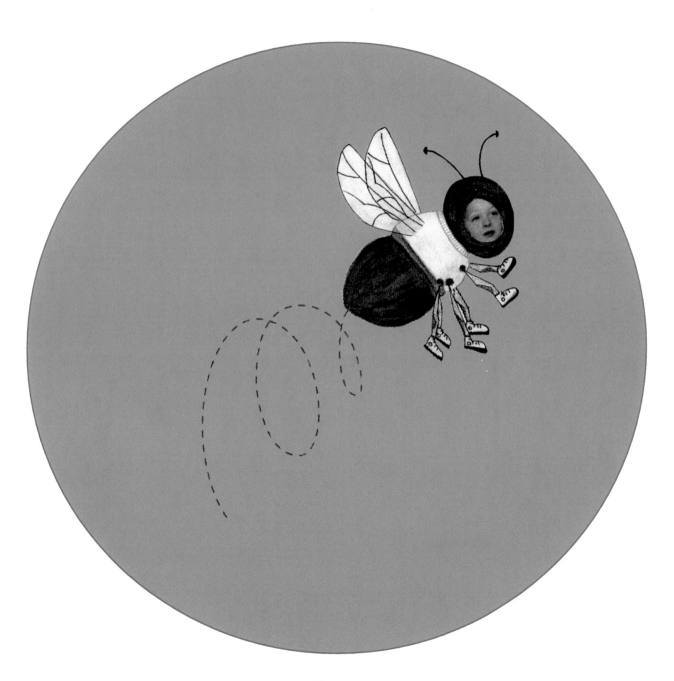

About The Author

Donald Gent, the author of **Ferdie the Fly** was a Midwestern boy, born and educated in Missouri. As a young adult, he resided in Kansas and then moved to Indiana with his wife and five children. One of the greatest pleasures was telling these interactive **Ferdie the Fly** stories to the children, grandchildren, and many other children who flapped their arms and went with **Ferdie** on his many adventures. The stories were compiled and illustrated by his daughter, Rachel, in memory of a great father, an engaging storyteller, and a man who brought a smile to many a child's face.

Made in the USA
Monee, IL
23 June 2022

98499522R00052